Cubic Measure

1728 cubic inches = 1 cubic foot

27 cubic feet = 1 cubic yard

128 cubic feet = 1 cord of wood

24 3/4 cubic feet = 1 perch of stone

NOTE: A cord of wood is a pile 8 feet long, 4 feet wide and 4 feet high. A perch of stone or brick is 16 1/2 feet wide and 1 foot high.

---

24 sheets = 1 quire
20 quires = 1 ream
10 reams = 1 bale

Volume

LITERS	PINTS	QUARTS	GAL.
1.000	2.113	1.057	.264
.473	1.000		1/8
.946	2.000	1.000	1/4
3.785	8.000	4.000	1.000

---

12 units = 1 dozen
12 dozen = 1 gross
12 gross = 1 great gross
20 units = 1 score
1 hand = 4 inches
1 fathom = 6 feet
1 knot = 6086 feet
3 knots = 1 league
1 bushel potatoes = 60 pounds
1 barrel flour = 196 pounds
1 cu. ft. of water = 7.48 liquid gal. and weighs 62.425 pounds.

CM	INCHES	FEET
1.00	.394	.0328
2.54	1.000	1/12
30.48	12.000	1.000

---

16 drams = 1 ounce

16 ounces = 1 pound

100 pounds = 1 hundredweight

2000 pounds = 1 ton

2240 pounds = 1 long ton

Misc. Measure

Diameter of a circle x 3.1416=the circumference.

Diameter of a circle squared x .7854=area.

Atmospheric pressure is 14.7 pounds per square inch at sea level.

13 1/2 cubic feet of air =1 pound

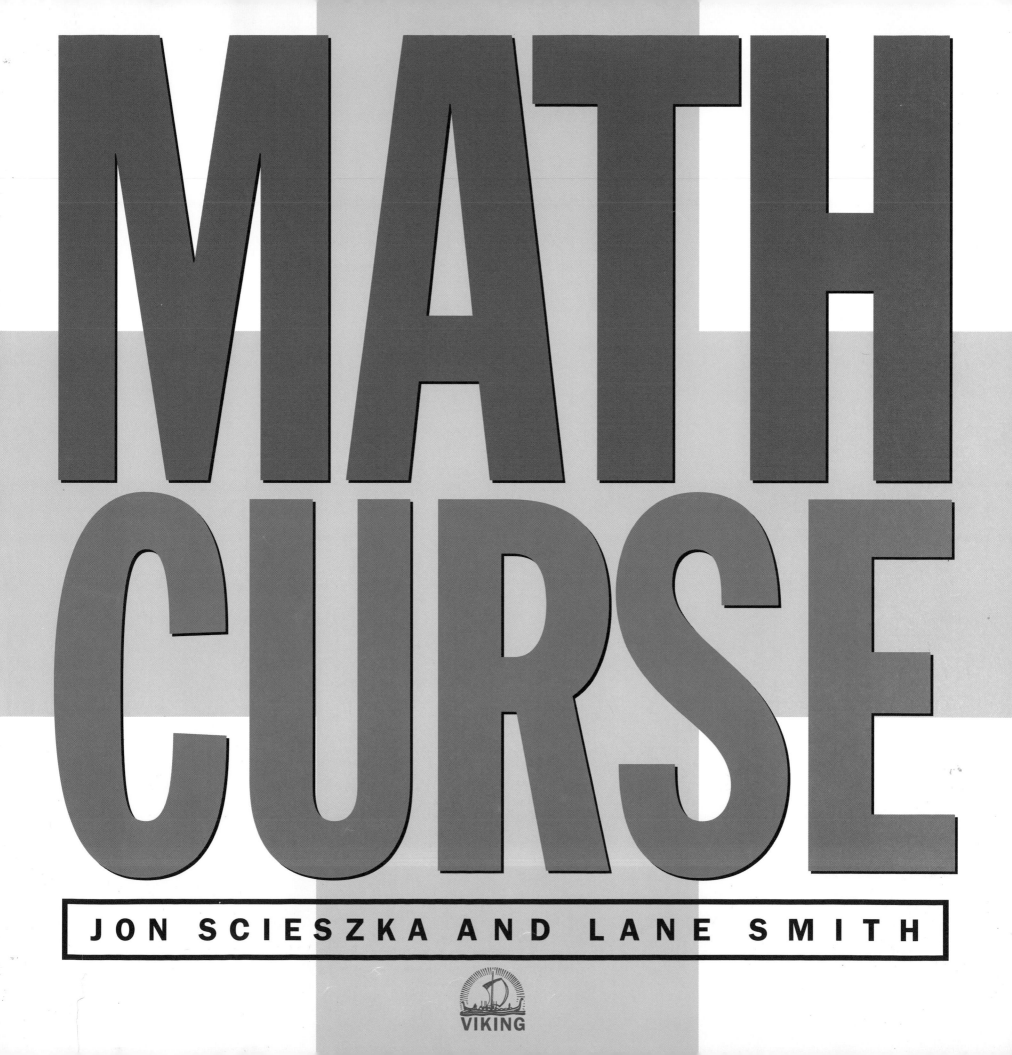

MATH CURSE

JON SCIESZKA AND LANE SMITH

VIKING

VIKING
Published by the Penguin Group
Penguin Books USA Inc., 375 Hudson Street, New York, New York 10014, USA
Penguin Books Ltd, 27 Wrights Lane, London W8 5TZ, England
Penguin Books Australia Ltd, Ringwood, Victoria, Australia
Penguin Books Canada Ltd, 10 Alcorn Avenue, Toronto, Ontario, Canada M4V 3B2
Penguin Books (N.Z.) Ltd, 182–190 Wairau Road, Auckland 10, New Zealand

Penguin Books Ltd, Registered Offices: Harmondsworth, Middlesex, England

First published in 1995 by Viking, a division of Penguin Books USA Inc.
3 5 7 9 10 8 6 4 2

LIBRARY OF CONGRESS CATALOGING-IN-PUBLICATION DATA
Scieszka, Jon.   Math curse/by Jon Scieszka; illustrated by Lane Smith.   p. cm.
Summary: When the teacher tells her class that they can think of almost everything as a math problem,
one student acquires a math anxiety which becomes a real curse.
ISBN 0-670-86194-4
[1. Math anxiety—Fiction.   2. Mathematics—Fiction.   3. Schools—Fiction.]   I. Smith, Lane, ill.   II. Title.
PZ7.S41267Mat 1995 [E]—dc20 95-12341 CIP AC
Printed in U.S.A.   Set in Franklin Gothic.

DESIGN: Molly Leach, New York, New York

All of the paintings were composed without using the golden section.

If the sum of my nieces and nephews equals 15, and their product equals 54, and I have more nephews than nieces, HOW MANY NEPHEWS AND HOW MANY NIECES IS THIS BOOK DEDICATED TO?

—J.S.

If I divide the number of years my dad was an accountant (30) by the number of years I needed help with my math (30), I get one (1) dedication: FOR DAD (THE C.P.A.)

—L.S.

ON MONDAY in math class,

Mrs. Fibonacci says,

"**YOU KNOW**, you can think
of almost everything
as a math problem."

On Tuesday I start having problems.

at 7:15. It takes me 10 minutes to get dressed,
15 minutes to eat my breakfast,
and 1 minute to brush my teeth.

SUDDENLY, it's a problem:

❶ If my bus leaves at 8:00,
will I make it on time?

❷ How many minutes
in 1 hour?

❸ How many teeth in
1 mouth?

I look in my
closet, and the
problems get worse:

I have 1 white shirt,
3 blue shirts, 3 striped shirts,
and that 1 ugly plaid shirt
my Uncle Zeno sent me.

❶ How many shirts is
that all together?

❷ How many shirts would
I have if I threw away
that awful plaid shirt?

❸ When will Uncle Zeno quit
sending me such ugly shirts?

I'M GETTING a little worried.

I TAKE the milk out for my cereal and wonder:

1. How many quarts in a gallon?
2. How many pints in a quart?
3. How many inches in a foot?
4. How many feet in a yard?
5. How many yards in a neighborhood? How many inches in a pint? How many feet in my shoes?

I don't even bother to take out the cereal. I don't want to know how many flakes in a bowl.

Mrs. Fibonacci has obviously put a

MATH CURSE

on me. Everything I look at or think about has become a math problem.

I TRY to get on the bus without thinking about anything, but there are 5 KIDS already on the bus, 5 KIDS get on at my stop, 5 MORE get on at the next stop, and 5 MORE get on at the last stop.

✔ **TRUE OR FALSE: What is the bus driver's name?**

6 6 5 2

5

BUS

OCT   NOV   DEC

DECEMBER

Mrs. Fibonacci has this **CHART**
of what month everyone's birthday is in:

❶ Which month has the
 most birthdays?

❷ Which month has the fewest?

❸ Why doesn't February have a *w*?

❹ Don't you think this chart looks
 sort of like a row of buildings?

❺ Do you ever look at clouds and
 think they look like something else?

❻ What does this inkblot
 look like to you?

THE WHOLE morning is one problem after another. There are **24 kids** in my class. I just know someone is going to bring in cupcakes to share. We sit in **4 rows** with **6 desks** in each row.

What if Mrs. Fibonacci rearranges the desks to make 6 rows?

8 rows?   3 rows?   2 rows?

I COUNT the 24 kids in our class again, this time by 2s.

Jake scratches his paper with one finger.
▶ **How many fingers are in our class?**
Casey pulls Eric's ear.
▶ **How many ears are in our class?**
The new girl, Kelly, sticks her tongue out at me.
▶ **How many tongues in our class?**

I'M about to really lose it, when the lunch bell rings.

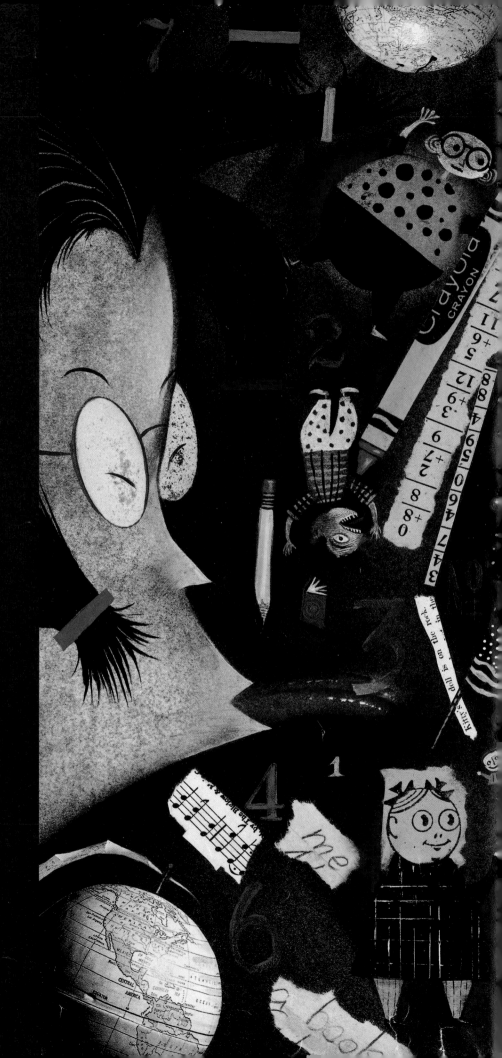

Unfortunately for me,
LUNCH is pizza and apple pie.
Each pizza is cut into 8 equal slices.
Each pie is cut into 6 equal slices.
And you know what that means:
fractions.

❶ If I want 2 slices of pizza should I ask for:

a. 1/8

b. 2/8

c. 2 slices of pizza

❷ What is another way to say 1/2 of an apple pie?

a. 2/6

b. 3/6

c. la moitié d'une tarte aux pommes

❸ Which tastes greater?

a. 1/2 a pizza

b. 1/2 an apple pie

We haven't studied fractions yet,
so I take 12 carrot sticks 3 at a time
and eat them 2 at a time.

In the afternoon, every subject is a problem.

SOCIAL STUDIES

is a geography problem:

The Mississippi River is about 4,000 kilometers long.

An M&M is about 1 centimeter long.

There are 100 centimeters in a meter, and 1,000 meters in a kilometer.

1 Estimate how many M&Ms it would take to measure the length of the Mississippi River.

2 Estimate how many M&Ms you would eat if you had to measure the Mississippi River with M&Ms.

BONUS: Can you spell Mississippi without any M&Ms?

ENGLISH is a word problem:

If mail + box = mailbox:

❶ Does lipstick – stick = lip?

❷ Does tunafish + tunafish = fournafish?

PHYS. ED. is a sports problem:

In 1919, Babe Ruth hit 29 home runs, batted .322, and made $40,000.

In 1991, the average major league baseball player hit 15 home runs, batted .275, and made $840,000.

☞ CIRCLE THE CORRECT ANSWER:

Babe Ruth < The average modern baseball player

Babe Ruth > The average modern baseball player

Babe Ruth = The average modern baseball player

MATH is just a total problem. Mrs. Fibonacci says there are many ways to count. She asks us to give some examples. Russell counts on his fingers: "1, 2, 3, 4, 5, 6, 7, 8, 9, 10."

Molly says: "2, 4, 6, 8, 10..."

Mrs. Fibonacci says:

"I always count 1, 1, 2, 3, 5, 8, 13...

"But on the planet **Tetra,**
kids have only 2 fingers on each hand.
They count **1, 2, 3, 10...**

"And on the planet **Binary,**
kids have only 1 finger on each hand.
They count **1, 10...**"

1 What are the next five numbers
in each sequence above?

2 Do you think Mrs. Fibonacci
has been to the planet Tetra?

3 How would you bowl if you lived
on the planet Binary?

We are just about to go home when Rebecca remembers the special birthday cupcakes her mom made.

There are 24 KIDS in the class.
Rebecca has 24 CUPCAKES.

✗ So what's the problem?

Rebecca wants Mrs. Fibonacci to have a cupcake, too.

Everyone is going crazy trying to figure out
what fraction of a cupcake each person will get.

I'm the first to figure out the answer.

I raise my hand and tell Mrs. Fibonacci
I'm allergic to cupcakes.

EVERYONE (24) believes me
and gets ONE (1) cupcake.
NO ONE (0) has to figure out fractions.

I stagger out of school.

I'm a math zombie now.
I have to find something to break this math curse.
I decide to try chocolate.
My favorite candy bar is usually 50¢.

But guess what?

Today it's on sale for 50% off:

$$\frac{-B \pm \sqrt{B^2 - 4AC}}{2A}$$

Where **A** = the number of letters in your first name, **B** = your age, and **C** = your shoe size

I decide to buy licorice instead.

I pull out my money.

I have a $5 bill, a $1 bill, a quarter, and a penny. George Washington is on both the quarter and the $1 bill. Abraham Lincoln is on both the penny and the $5 bill.

✔ SO WHICH IS TRUE:

a. 1 Washington equals 25 Lincolns.
b. 5 Washingtons equal 1 Lincoln.
c. 1 Washington equals 100 Lincolns.
d. 1 Lincoln equals 20 Washingtons.

Don't forget to show your work.

EXTRA CREDIT: How do you think Thomas Jefferson feels about all of this?

I am now a raving math lunatic.
What if this keeps up for a whole year?
How many minutes of math madness would that be?
"What's your problem?" says my sister.
"365 days x 24 hours x 60 minutes," I snarl.

Dinner brings no relief.
While passing the mashed potatoes,
Mom says, "What your father says is false."
Dad helps himself to some potatoes and says,
"What your mother says is true."
I think about that for a minute.
If what Mom says is true, then what Dad says is false.
But if what Dad says is false, then what Mom says isn't true.
And if what Mom says isn't true, then what Dad says isn't false.
But that can't be true because he says that what
Mom says is true, and she says that what he says is false.

Can that be true?
I think about that. Then I think about it some more.
Then I think I'd better go to bed.

I undo 8 buttons plus 2 shoelaces.
I subtract 2 shoes.
I multiply times 2 socks and divide by 3 pillows to get 5 sheep,
remainder 1, which is all I need to count before I fall asleep.

Then the problems really begin.

I DREAM I'm trapped in a room with no doors and no windows.

Fractions. I break the chalk in half. Then I put the two halves together. One half plus one half equals one whole.

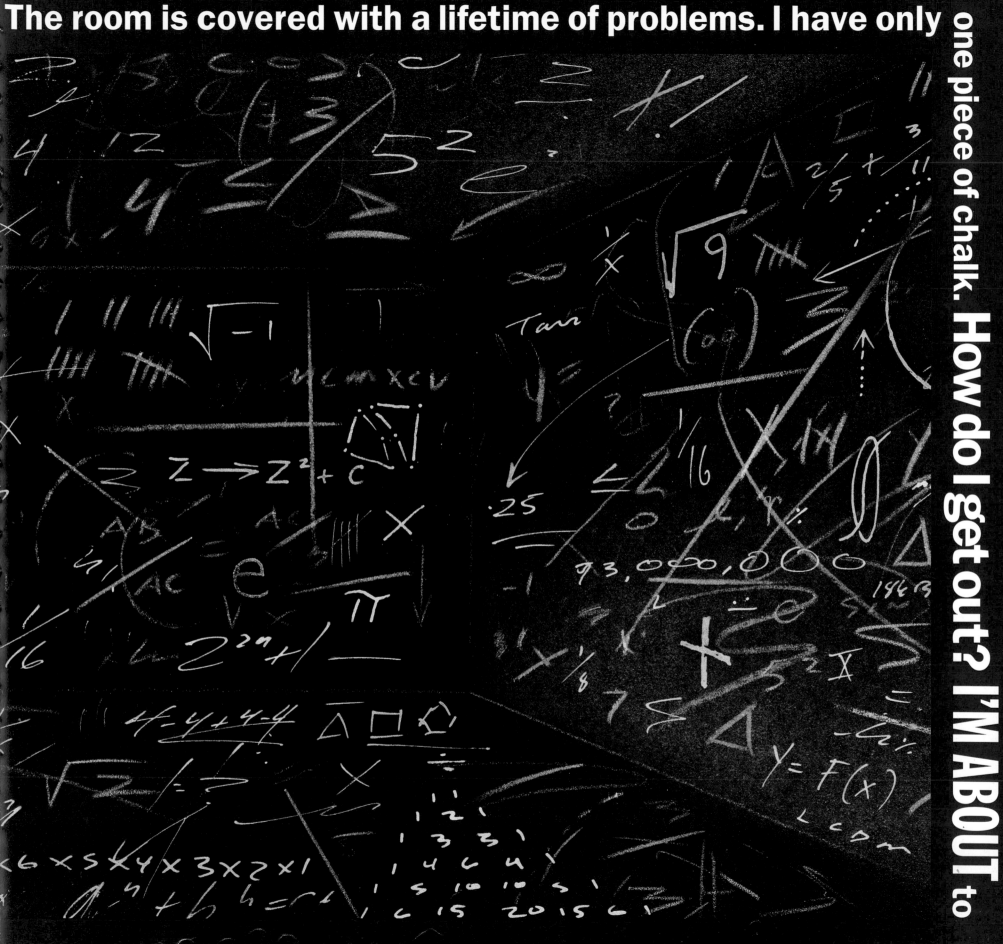

I put the hole on the wall and jump out.

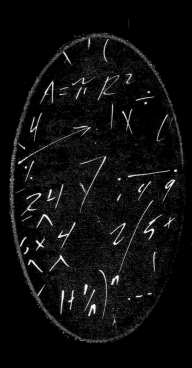

I'M FREE.

I wake up

Wednesday morning at 7:15.

It takes me 10 minutes to get dressed,
15 minutes to eat my breakfast,
and 1 minute to brush my teeth.
My bus leaves at 8:00.

What time will I be ready?

 **7:41**

NO PROBLEM.

I've broken the math curse.

I can solve any problem.

And life is just great until science class, when

Mr. Newton says,

"**YOU KNOW**, you can think of almost everything as a science experiment..."

Multiplication Table

1	2	3	4	5	6	7	8	9	10
2	4	6	8	10	12	14	16	18	20
3	6	9	12	15	18	21	24	27	30
4	8	12	16	20	24	28	32	36	40
5	10	15	20	25	30	35	40	45	50
6	12	18	24	30	36	42	48	54	60
7	14	21	28	35	42	49	56	63	70
8	16	24	32	40	48	56	64	72	80
9	18	27	36	45	54	63	72	81	90
10	20	30	40	50	60	70	80	90	100

Conversions

Meters	Yards	Inches
1.000	1.093	39.37
.914	1.000	36.00

GRAMS	OUNCES	POUNDS
1.00	.035	.002
28.35	1.000	1/16
453.59	16.00	1.000
1000.00	35.274	2.205

Measure

144 sq. in. = 1 sq. ft.
9 sq. ft. = 1 sq. yd.
30 1/4 sq. yds. = 1 sq. rod
160 sq. rods = 1 acre
640 acres = 1 sq. mile
An acre measures
208.71 ft. on each side.
A section of land is 1 sq. mile.
A quarter section is 160 acres.
A township is 36 sq. miles.

Surface Measure

1 METER = 100 CM
100 CM = 1,000 MM
1 MM = .001 M
1 CM = .01 M
1 DM = .1 M
1 DAM = 10 M
1 HM = 100 M
1 KM = 1,000 M

Time Measure

60 seconds = 1 minute
60 minutes = 1 hour
24 hours = 1 day
7 days = 1 week
30 days = 1 calendar month
12 months = 1 year
365 days = 1 common year
366 days = 1 leap year
100 years = 1 century